D1230435

DISCARDED

Editors: Ann Redpath, Etienne Delessert
Art Director: Rita Marshall
Publisher: George R. Peterson, Jr.

Copyright © 1983 Creative Education, Inc., 123 S. Broad Street,
Mankato, Minnesota 56001, USA. American Edition.
Copyright © 1983 Grasset & Fasquelle, Paris – Editions 24 Heures, Lausanne. French Edition.
International copyrights reserved in all countries.

Library of Congress Catalog Card No.: 83-71174
Norwegian Fairy Tale; Bushy Bride
Mankato, MN: Creative Education, Inc.; 32 pages. ISBN: 0-87191-952-4

Printed in Switzerland by Imprimeries Réunies S.A. Lausanne.

BUSHY BRIDE

NORWEGIAN FAIRY TALE
illustrated by
SEYMOUR CHWAST

8882

CREATIVE EDUCATION INC.

ONCE UPON A TIME

THERE was a widower who
had a son and a daughter by
his first wife. They were both
good children, and loved each
other with all their hearts. After
some time had gone by, the
man married again, and he
chose a widow with one daughter who was ugly and wicked,
and her mother was ugly and
wicked too. From the very day
that the new wife came into the
house, there was no peace for
the man's children, and not a
corner to be found where they
could get any rest. So the boy
thought that the best thing he
could do was to go out into
the world and try to earn his
own bread.

When he had roamed about
for some time he came to the
King's palace, where he ob-
tained a place under the coach-
man; and very brisk and active
he was, and the horses that he
looked after were so fat and
sleek, that they shone again.

But his sister, who was still at home, fared worse and worse. Both her stepmother and her stepsister were always finding fault with her, whatever she did and wherever she went. And they scolded her and abused her so that she never had an hour's peace. They made her do all the hard work, and hard words fell to her lot early and late, but little enough food accompanied them.

One day they sent her to the brook to fetch some water home, and an ugly and horrible head rose up out of the water, and said, "Wash me, girl!"

"Yes, I will wash you with pleasure," said the girl, and began to wash and scrub the ugly face, but she couldn't help thinking that it was a very unpleasant piece of work. When she had done it, and done it well,

another head rose up out of the water, and this one was uglier still.

"Brush me, girl!" said the head.

"Yes, I will brush you with pleasure," said the girl, and set to work with the tangled hair, and, as may be easily imagined, this too was by no means very pleasant work.

When she had gotten it done, another and a much more ugly and horrible-looking head rose up out of the water.

"Kiss me, girl!" said the head.

"Yes, I will kiss you," said the man's daughter, and she did it, but she thought it was the worst bit of work that she had ever had to do in her life.

So the heads all began to talk to each other, and to ask what they should do for this girl who was so full of kindliness.

"She shall be the prettiest girl that ever was, and fair and bright as the day," said the first head.

"Gold shall drop from her hair whenever she brushes it," said the second.

"Gold shall drop from her mouth whenever she speaks," said the third head.

So when the man's daughter went home, looking as beautiful and bright as day, the stepmother and her daughter grew much more ill-tempered, and it was worse still when she began to talk, and they saw that golden coins dropped from her mouth. The stepmother fell into such a towering passion that she drove the man's daughter into the pigsty. She might stay there with her fine show of gold, the stepmother said, but she should not be permitted to set foot in the house.

It was not long before the mother wanted her own daughter to go to the stream to fetch some water.

When she got there with her pails, the first head rose up out of the water close to the bank.

"Wash me, girl!" it said.

"Wash yourself!" answered the woman's daughter.

Then the second head came up out of the water.

"Brush me, girl!" said the head.

"Brush yourself!" said the girl.

So down it went to the bottom, and the third head came up.

"Kiss me, girl!" said the head.

"As if I would kiss your ugly mouth!" said the girl.

So again the heads talked together about what they should do for this girl who was so ill-tempered and full of her own importance, and they agreed that she should have a nose that was four ells long, and a jaw that was three ells, and a fir bush in the middle of her forehead, and every time she spoke ashes should fall from her mouth.

When she came back to the cottage door with her pails, she called to her mother who was inside, "Open the door!"

"Open the door yourself, my own dear child!" said the mother.

"I can't get near, because of my nose," said the daughter.

When the mother came and saw her you may imagine what a state of mind she was in, and how she screamed and lamented, but neither the nose nor the jaw grew any the less for that.

Now the brother, who was in service in the King's palace, had taken a portrait of his sister, and he had carried the picture away with him. Every morning and evening he knelt down before it and prayed for his sister, so dearly did he love her.

The other stableboys had heard him doing this, so they peeped through the keyhole into his room, and saw that he was kneeling there before a picture. They told everyone that every morning and evening the youth knelt down and prayed to an idol which he had. And at last they went to the King himself, and begged that he too would peep through the keyhole, and see for himself what the youth did. At first the King would not believe this. But after a long, long time, they prevailed upon him, and he crept on tiptoe to the door, peeped through, and saw the youth on his knees, with his hands clasped together before a picture which was hanging on the wall.

"Open the door!" cried the King, but the youth did not hear.

So the King called to him again, but the youth was praying so fervently that he did not hear him this time either.

"Open the door, I say!" cried the King again. "It is I! I want to come in."

So the youth sprang to the door and unlocked it, but in his haste he forgot to hide the picture.

When the King entered and saw it, he stood still as if he were in fetters, and could not stir from the spot, for the picture seemed to him so beautiful.

"There is nowhere on earth so beautiful a woman as this!" said the King.

But the youth told him that she was his sister, and that he had painted her, and that if she was not prettier than the picture, she was at all events not uglier.

"Well, if she is as beautiful as that, I will have her for my Queen," said the King, and he commanded the youth to go home and fetch her without a moment's delay, and to lose no time in coming back.

The youth promised to make all the haste he could, and set forth from the King's palace.

When the brother arrived at home to fetch his sister, her stepmother and stepsister wanted to go too. So they all set out together, and the man's daughter took with her a casket in which she kept her gold, and a dog which was called Little Snow. These two things were all that she had inherited from her mother. When they had traveled for some time they had to cross the sea. The brother sat down at the helm, and the mother and the two stepsisters went to the forepart of the vessel, and they sailed a long, long way.

At last they came in sight of land.

"Look at that white strand there; that is where we shall land," said the brother, pointing across the sea.

"What is my brother saying?" inquired the man's daughter.

"He says that you are to throw your casket out into the sea," answered the stepmother.

"Well, if my brother says so, I must do it," said the man's daughter, and she flung her casket into the sea.

When they had sailed for some time longer, the brother once more pointed over the sea.

"There you may see the palace to which we are bound," said he.

"What is my brother saying?" asked the man's daughter.

"Now he says that you are to throw your dog into the sea," answered the stepmother.

The man's daughter wept, and was sorely troubled, for Little Snow was the dearest thing she had on earth, but at last she threw him overboard.

"If my brother says that, I must do it, but Heaven knows how unwilling I am to throw thee out, Little Snow!" said she.

So they sailed onwards a long way farther.

"There you may see the King coming out to meet you," said the brother, pointing to the seashore.

"What is my brother saying?" asked his sister again.

"Now he says that you are to make haste and throw yourself overboard," answered the stepmother.

She wept and she wailed, but as her brother had said that, she thought she must do it. So she leaped into the sea.

When they arrived at the palace, and the King beheld the ugly bride with a nose that was four ells long, a jaw that was three ells, and a forehead that had a bush in the middle of it, he was quite terrified. But the wedding feast was all prepared, as regarded brewing and baking, and all the wedding guests were sitting waiting, so, ugly as she was, the King was forced to take her.

But he was very wroth, and none can blame him for that; so he caused the brother to be thrown into a pit full of snakes.

On the first Thursday night after this, a beautiful maiden came into the kitchen of the palace, and begged the kitchen maid, who slept there, to lend her a brush. She begged very prettily, and got it, and then she brushed her hair, and the gold dropped from it.

A little dog was with her, and she said to it, "Go out, Little Snow, and see if it will soon be day!"

This she said thrice, and the third time that she sent out the dog to see, it was very near dawn. Then she was forced to depart, but as she went she said:

"Out on thee,
Ugly Bushy Bride,
Sleeping so soft
By the young King's side,
On sand and stones,
My bed I make,
And my brother sleeps
With the cold snake,
Unpitied and unwept."

"I shall come twice more, and then never again," said she.

In the morning the kitchen maid related what she had seen and heard, and the King said that next Thursday night he himself would watch in the kitchen and see if this were true, and when it had begun to grow dark he went out into the kitchen to the girl. But though he rubbed his eyes and did everything he could to keep himself awake it was all in vain, for the Bushy Bride crooned and sang till his eyes were fast closed. When the beautiful young maiden came he was sound asleep and snoring.

This time also, as before, she borrowed a brush and brushed her hair with it, and the gold dropped down as she did it. And again she sent the dog out three times, and when day dawned she departed. But as she was going she said as she had said before, "I shall come once more, and then never again."

On the third Thursday night the King once more insisted on keeping watch. Then he set two men to hold him; each of them was to take an arm, and shake him and jerk him by the arm whenever he seemed to be going to fall asleep. He set two men to watch his Bushy Bride. But as the night wore on the Bushy Bride again began to croon and to sing, so that his eyes began to close and his head to droop on one side. Then came the lovely maiden, and got the brush and brushed her hair till the gold dropped from it, and then she sent her Little Snow out to see if it would soon be day, and this she did three times. The third time it was just beginning to grow light, and then she said:

> "Out on thee,
> Ugly Bushy Bride,
> Sleeping so soft
> By the young King's side,
> On sand and stones
> My bed I make,
> And my brother sleeps
> With the cold snake,
> Unpitied and unwept."

"Now I shall never come again," she said, and then she turned to go. But the two men who were holding the King by the arms seized his hands and forced a knife into his grasp, and then made him cut her little finger just enough to make it bleed.

Thus the true bride was freed. The King then awoke, and she told him all that had taken place, and how her stepmother and stepsister had betrayed her. Then the brother was at once taken out of the snake pit–the snakes had never touched him–and the stepmother and stepsister were flung down into it instead of him.

No one can tell how delighted the King was to get rid of that hideous Bushy Bride, and get a Queen who was bright and beautiful as day itself.

And now the real wedding was held, and held in such a way that it was heard of and spoken about all over seven kingdoms. The King and his bride drove to church, and Little Snow was in the carriage too. When the blessing was given they went home again, and after that I saw no more of them.